Fingerplay Friends

Action Rhymes
for
Home, Church, and School

Audrey Olson Leighton

Judson Press® Valley Forge

Acknowledgments and Credits

"There Was a Little Turtle," by Vachel Lindsay, from *Collected Poems of Vachel Lindsay*. Copyright 1920 by Macmillan Co., Inc. Renewed 1948 by Elizabeth C. Lindsay. Reprinted with permission of Macmillan Publishing Company.

"The Beehive," by Emilie Poulsson, from *Finger Plays for Nursery and Kindergarten*, published by Lothrop, Lee & Shepard Co., copyright 1893.

Many of the poems are from nursery rhymes and poems that have been traditionally used with children. In some cases where poems have not been acknowledged, we have searched diligently to find sources but without success.

FINGERPLAY FRIENDS
Copyright © 1984
Judson Press, Valley Forge, PA 19482-0851

Library of Congress Cataloging in Publication Data
Main entry under title:
Fingerplay friends.
    Includes indexes.
    1. Finger plays. 2. Nursery rhymes. 3. Children's
poetry. I. Leighton, Audrey Olson.
GV1218.F5F56 1984   793.4   84-9707
ISBN 0-8170-1051-3

The name JUDSON PRESS is registered as a trademark in the U.S. Patent Office.
Printed in the U.S.A. ⊕

Lovingly, to Don, Echo, and Karla

Table of Contents

In the Church

Animal Adventures

Friends and Family

Toys and Tools

In the Garden

Hurrah for Holidays

The Spell of Seasons

Preface

Dear Friends of Children,

Fingerplay Friends was compiled for parents, teachers, and other friends of children to provide a source of fingerplays that children have found enjoyable and educational. Some are new but many, such as "This Is the Church," are old favorites.

Fingerplays hold a number of values for children. One of the foremost values is language development. A child's first year of life is the most important year in the development of listening language. Babies are fascinated with the beat of the words as they hear the poems. Parents and teachers have naturally added actions to the words to help young children learn their meaning. When the hand action is added to the rhyme, children pay attention. Soon young children will add the action when they hear the poem, even before they are able to speak. The frequent repeating of fingerplays is of great value in learning a language as the wide variety of sounds in a language requires repetition to learn.

Fingerplays provide fun ways to learn the names for parts of the body, animals, colors, or plants. In addition to the development of vocabulary, various concepts of size, feelings, space, place, numbers, or time can be presented by fingerplays.

Language development is further aided by hearing the sentences of fingerplays. Poetry provides a new source of language that is different from everyday talk.

As children grow, they begin to feed and dress themselves, draw, and write. All of these tasks use hands and fingers. The ability to use hands and fingers improves with the practice provided in fingerplays.

Children's ability to listen grows as they listen for the words so that they can add the action at the right time. As a result their attention span grows as well.

A child's ability to talk is aided as fingerplays help in pronouncing words and in forming sentences. Children use make-believe as they act out various fingerplays, and thus they have an early introduction to drama.

When to Use Fingerplays

The times for sharing fingerplays with a young child or infant are many and varied. Fingerplays may be used whenever they fit into what is happening or they may be done at a scheduled time each day. They may be used at various times, such as when holding a child on your lap, when reading a book, bathing an infant, riding in a car, changing a diaper, etc.

Fingerplays may help a young child get acquainted with a new adult in his or her life. If a new baby-sitter knows the same fingerplays that the child's parents know, he or she then approaches the child with something familiar. Grandparents also appreciate knowing what fingerplays are familiar to a child.

In addition to being used individually with young children, fingerplays can also be used with groups of preschool children. They may be used to draw children together for story time. Many teachers use fingerplays to introduce or to follow up on a book that they are reading to the class.

After a period of time, small children need a change from sitting quietly. A fingerplay helps to relieve their restlessness and prepares them for the next story or prayer time. The more active fingerplays help to use up a child's energy.

A new color may be introduced to a preschool class with a fingerplay. "The Traffic Light" may be used to teach safety in walking to school. The subject index will be helpful for teachers and parents who are looking for a fingerplay on a certain topic.

Games may be played around fingerplays. Class discussions may be initiated after hearing and doing a fingerplay. A fingerplay may be used to reinforce a request: "A Cold" encourages covering a sneeze, and "Listening Time" invites quietness.

Fingerplays are also used with children of school age. Many teachers use the fingerplays that involve some type of counting for this age group. Prereading and reading skills are encouraged as children "read" a fingerplay they know. Older children are encouraged to write their own fingerplays.

Students who have a hearing loss find fingerplays helpful. The teacher is saying the words, and the fingers act out the meaning very much like the sign language for the deaf. Some of the actions in this book use the sign language for the deaf. When deaf sign language is used, it will be indicated with the initials "D.S.L.," followed by the word it shows.

Teachers who teach English as a second language frequently use fingerplays to explain the meaning of words. The Indian sign for "friend" is used in the fingerplay "Thanksgiving Friends."

Hints for Using Fingerplays

Here are some basic hints for using fingerplays. Short rhymes and simple actions are best for young children. Children like rhymes that repeat words and that set a beat.

When teaching a new fingerplay, read the poem aloud. Then resay it and add the actions. Repeat one line at a time until the children know that line. Many young children are more comfortable doing only the actions before saying the words. Introduce only one new fingerplay at a time.

The hand or body actions should be kept as simple as possible. Do not add too many actions for any one line of the poem. The actions should suit the words and flow with the rhythm. If any of the actions suggested in this book seem awkward, change them. Also change the fingerplay words to fit a new situation.

If a fingerplay contains a word that the children do not know, give a brief explanation or simply show them. For example, touch a shoulder and say, "This is your shoulder."

Pronounce the words carefully and with a good deal of expression. Lowering the volume of your voice helps to quiet a group.

Teachers and parents may wish to change any fingerplays that they feel stereotype a group or an individual.

May you and your children find this collection of fingerplays helpful and fun. A fingerplay provides mutual interaction between a child and a caring adult. A fingerplay is a gift of time shared with a child.

Lovingly,

Audrey Leighton

The Child from Head to Toe

Right Hand, Left Hand

This is my right hand;
I'll raise it up high.
    (*lift right hand over head*)

This is my left hand;
I'll touch the sky.
    (*lift left hand*)

Right hand, left hand,
    (*show right hand, then left*)

Roll them around.
    (*roll hands over each other*)

Left hand, right hand,
    (*show left hand, then right*)

Pound, pound, pound.
    (*hit fists together*)

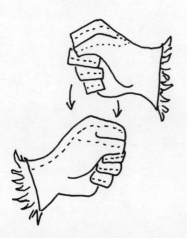

Sleep Time

Cat's in the corner,
  *(place hands on either side of the mouth
  and pretend to stroke whiskers—
  D.S.L. for cat)*
Bird's in the tree,
  (move arms like flying)
Goodnight to all,
  (wave good-bye)
It's sleep time for me.
  (cover a yawn)

Left to the Window

Left to the window,
  (left hand point at window)
Right to the door,
  (right hand point at door)
Up to the ceiling,
  (arms reach up)
Down to the floor.
  (bend down to floor)

15

Head and Shoulders

Head and shoulders,
Knees and toes.
Head and shoulders,
Knees and toes.

Eyes and ears,
And mouth and nose.
Head and shoulders,
Knees and toes.
*(touch each body part
as mentioned; repeat
faster and faster)*

Touch My Hair

I touch my hair, my lips, my eyes.
I sit up straight; then I rise.
I touch my ears, my nose, my chin,
And then I sit back down again.
(follow actions as rhyme indicates)

Thumbkin Says, "I'll Dance"

Thumbkin says, "I'll dance."
Thumbkin says, "I'll dance."
Dancing, singing, merry little one,
Thumbkin says, "I'll dance again."
(bounce thumbs up and down on table)

Repeat the rhyme with: Pointer, Tall One, Ring One, Little One, and finally All Fingers.

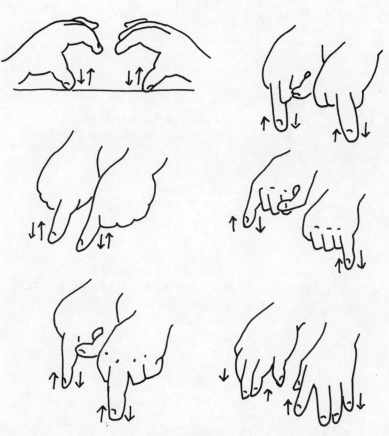

Ten Fingers

I have ten little fingers,
And they all belong to me.
(hold hands out in front)

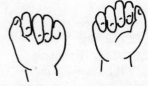

I can make them do things,
Would you like to see?
I can shut them up tight.
(make a fist)

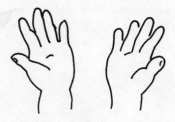

I can open them up wide.
(spread fingers out)

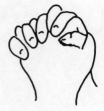

I can put them together.
(clasp hands together)

I can make them all hide.
(put hands behind back)

I can make them jump high.
(*raise hands over head*)

I can make them jump low.
(*lower hands to knees*)

I can fold them like this
And hold them just so.
(*fold hands on lap*)

Open Them, Shut Them

Open them, shut them,
Give a little clap.
Open them, shut them,
Lay them in your lap.
Creep them, creep them,
Right up to your chin.
Open wide your mouth,
But do not let them in!

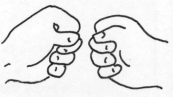

Open them, shut them,
Give a little clap.
Open them, shut them,
Lay them in your lap.
Creep them, creep them,
Right up to your cheek.
Put them over your eyes,
And through your fingers peek.
    (follow actions as rhyme indicates)

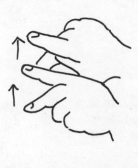

20

This Is Narrow

This is narrow.
  (*hold hands close together*)
This is wide.
  (*spread hands wide apart*)
Something else I know beside;
Up here is where my head is, you see.
  (*touch head*)
Down here is where my feet should be.
  (*touch feet*)

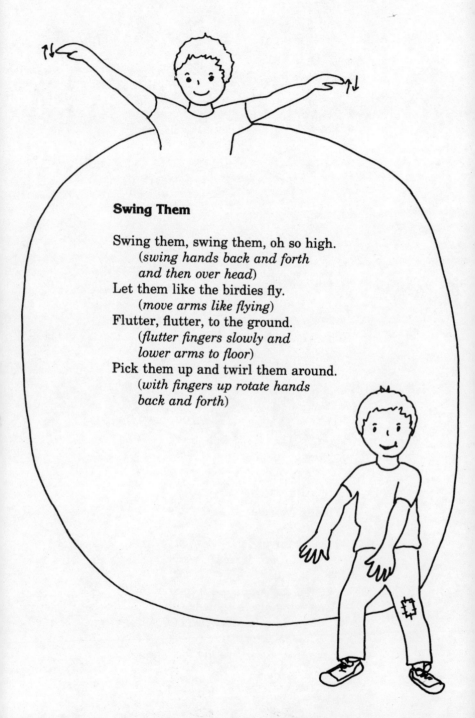

Swing Them

Swing them, swing them, oh so high.
   (*swing hands back and forth*
   and then over head)
Let them like the birdies fly.
   (*move arms like flying*)
Flutter, flutter, to the ground.
   (*flutter fingers slowly and*
   lower arms to floor)
Pick them up and twirl them around.
   (*with fingers up rotate hands*
   back and forth)

Hands on Shoulders

Hands on shoulders, hands on knees,
Hands behind you, if you please.
Touch your shoulders, now your nose,
Now your hair, and now your toes.

Hands up high in the air,
Down at your sides, and touch your hair.
Hands up high as before.
Now clap your hands—one, two, three, four.
(*follow actions as rhyme indicates*)

Roll, Roll, Roll Your Hands

Roll, roll, roll your hands,
As slowly as you can.

Roll, roll, roll your hands,
As slowly as you can.

Roll, roll, roll your hands,
As fast as you can.
    (*follow actions as rhyme indicates*)

The rhyme is repeated with verses 2 and 3:

(Verse 2) Shake, shake, shake your hands, etc.

(Verse 3) Clap, clap, clap your hands, etc.

Angry Volcano!

The little mountain was quiet and asleep,
All covered with snow so white and deep.
   (*children kneel down on floor*)

Then slowly the little mountain began to wake;
It started to rumble, and it started to shake.
   (*shake body slowly*)

Inside it grew so angry and hot!
Look out, top! You're going to pop!
   (*leap up quickly with arms up*)

A variation is to use a large box. The children take turns kneeling down in the box and "erupting." This may help to work out angry feelings or the fear of volcanoes.

My Hands upon My Head I Place

My hands upon my head I place,
Upon my shoulders, upon my face.
At my waist and by my side,
And then behind me they will hide.

Then I raise them way up high,
And let my fingers swiftly fly.
Then clap one, two, three,
And see how quiet they can be.
   (*follow actions as rhyme indicates*)

Listening Time

Sometimes my hands are at my side;
Then behind my back they hide.
Sometimes I wiggle fingers so,
Shake them fast, shake them slow.
Sometimes my hands go clap, clap, clap.
Then I rest them in my lap.
Now they're quiet as can be.
Because it's listening time, you see!
    (follow actions as rhyme indicates)

Clap with Me, One, Two, Three

Clap with me, one, two, three;
Clap, clap, clap, just like me.
Shake with me, one, two, three;
Shake, shake, shake, just like me.
Roll with me, one, two, three;
Roll, roll, roll, just like me.
Snap with me, one, two, three;
Snap, snap, snap, just like me.
Fold with me, one, two, three;
Now let them rest quietly.
    (follow actions as rhyme indicates)

Two Little Hands

Two little hands,
So clean and bright.
    (put hands behind you)
This is my left;
    (hold left hand up)
This is my right.
    (now bring right hand up)

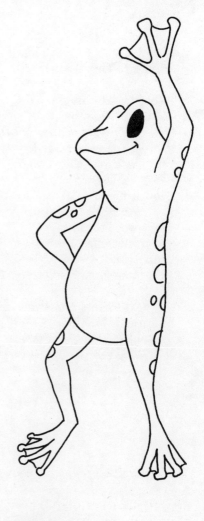

This Is My Right Foot

This is my right foot;
This is my left.
    (touch right and left feet)
And onto the floor they go.
They step together,
And keep the time,
So and so and so!
    (tap feet to time)

Where Is Thumbkin?

Where is Thumbkin?
Where is Thumbkin?
    (*put hands behind back*)
Here I am; here I am.
    (*show one thumb and
    then the other*)
How are you today, sir?
    (*bend one thumb*)
Very well, I thank you.
    (*bend other thumb*)
Run away, run away.
    (*hide hands behind back*)

    *The rhyme is repeated with:
Pointer, Tall One, Ring
Finger, Pinky, and then
All Fingers.*

In the Nursery

Peekaboo

Peekaboo, I see you!
If I see you, then you see me.
If you see me, then I see you.
Peekaboo, peekaboo.
   (*hide face behind hands
   and peek out*)

Duke of York

Oh, the grand old Duke of York,
Had ten thousand men.
He marched them up to the top of a hill.
   (*walk fingers from shoulder to
   top of child's head*)
Then he marched them down again.
   (*walk fingers back down to shoulder*)
When they were up, they were up,
   (*repeat walk to top of head*)
And when they were down, they were down.
   (*return walk to shoulder*)
But when they were halfway up,
   (*gently pinch child's nose*)
They were neither up nor down!

   *An alternate action may be to have the child
stand and sit as indicated.*

Pat-a-Cake

Pat-a-cake, pat-a-cake,
Baker's man.
Make me a cake,
As fast as you can.
    (*clap to rhythm of words*)
Pat it and prick it,
And mark it with B.*
    (*pretend to make in
    palm of hand*)
And put it in the oven,
For baby** and me.
    (*extend arms as though
    putting cake in oven*)

*Substitute your child's initial.
**Substitute your child's name.

A Cold

My nose can't smell;
    (*pinch nose*)
My head is hurting;
    (*touch head*)
I don't feel well;
    (*shake head*)
But when I sneeze,
    (*pretend to sneeze*)
I catch my sneeze,
If you please!
    (*cover mouth*)

This Little Pig

This little pig went to market,
(*touch big toe*)
This little pig stayed home.
(*touch next toe*)
This little pig had roast beef.
(*touch middle toe*)
This little pig had none.
(*touch next toe*)
This little pig said, "Wee,
Wee, wee," all the way home.
(*squeeze the little toe
and quickly run fingers
up leg to knee*)

Little Canary Yellow-Breast

Little Canary Yellow-Breast,
Sat upon a rail.
>   (*thumb and little finger up—
>   D.S.L. for yellow*)

Niddle-naddle went his head;
>   (*move thumb*)

Wiggle-waggle went his tail.
>   (*move little finger*)

Little Miss Muffet

Little Miss Muffet
>   (*run thumb down side of face—
>   D.S.L. for girl*)

Sat on a tuffet,
>   (*put one fist on top of other*)

Eating her curds and whey.
>   (*pretend to eat*)

Along came a spider
>   (*put one hand over the other
>   and lock little fingers—
>   D.S.L. for spider*)

And sat down beside her
>   (*move hands down, wiggle fingers*)

And frightened Miss Muffet away!
>   (*hide hands behind back*)

Humpty Dumpty

Humpty Dumpty sat on the wall;
   (*sit on the floor; hold
   child on lap*)
Humpty Dumpty had a great fall.
   (*rock back and forth; then
   slowly fall to one side*)
All the King's horses,
And all the King's men,
Couldn't put Humpty together again.
   (*slowly sit up*)

Little Bo-Peep

Little Bo-Peep has lost her sheep!
   (*hold hands over eyes and look around*)
And can't tell where to find them.
   (*hold hands behind back*)
Leave them alone and they will come home,
   (*bring hands from behind back*)
Wagging their tails behind them.
   (*wiggle little fingers*)

In the Church

Golden Rule

Dear God, help me now,
"To do to others as I would
That they should do to me."
To be gentle, kind, and good,
As Jesus showed us to be.
    (*hold hands in prayer gesture*)

Here Is the Church

Here is the church,
   (*interlace fingers to
   the inside of hands*)
And here is the steeple.
   (*raise and touch index fingers*)
Open the door
   (*spread thumbs apart*)
And see all the people.
   (*turn hands palms out with fingers raised*)
Here is the choir going upstairs,
   (*walk fingers of one hand over the other*)
And here is the minister leading in prayer.
   (*hold hands in prayer gesture*)

Little Baby Moses

Little baby Moses,
In the rushes did float,
Rocking gently back and forth,
Sleeping in his cradle boat.
    (*fold arms and rock them*
    back and forth)

Miriam, his sister kind,
Sang a quiet song,
As sitting by the rushes,
She watched all day long.
    (*place hand over eyes as*
    though watching)

Children Here and There

When it's dark nighttime here for me,
  (*cover eyes*)
Far away over the sea,
  (*wiggle fingers like water*)
On the other side of the world, it's day.
  (*open arms wide*)
There children like me run and play.
  (*point to self*)
The Lord loves children here and there.
  (*point to floor and then away*)
Love holds us all in God's care.
  (*cup hands together*)

Wiggles

I wiggle my fingers,
I wiggle my toes,
I wiggle my shoulders,
I wiggle my nose.
  (*follow action as indicated*)
Now no more wiggles
Are left in me.
  (*whisper*)
So I sit in church as
Still as can be.
  (*fold hands*)

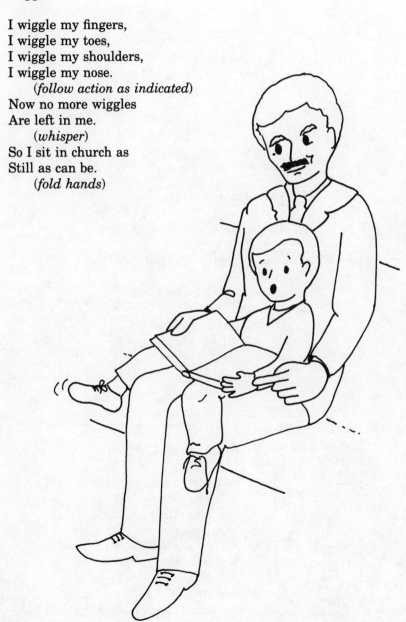

Children and Jesus

The children ran to see Jesus one day,
    (*run fingers up arm*)
But the men said, "Stop, take the
children away."
    (*hold palm up for stop sign*)
But Jesus said, "Let the children come."
    (*open arms wide and then close as in a hug*)
"I love children each and everyone."
    (*draw the outline of heart on chest—D.S.L.*
    for heart)

Jesus Loved Children

Jesus loved children, one and all,
    (*open arms wide*)
The ones still very small,
    (*indicate small children*
    with hands down to knees)
And the ones my size,
    (*point to self*)
And the ones so big and tall.
    (*raise hands high over head*)

Your* Lullaby

Sleep, sleep, sleep,
Baby,* so dear.
Sleep, sleep, sleep,
Mommy** is near.

Sleep, sleep, sleep,
God loves you.
Sleep, sleep, sleep,
Mommy** does too.
    (rock baby back and forth)

*Use your baby's name.
**Use Daddy, Grandma, etc.

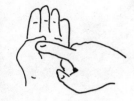

Off to Church

This little boy is going to bed,
 *(place pointer finger of one hand
 in palm of other hand)*
Down on the pillow he lays his head.
 *(thumb is pillow; place pointer finger
 on thumb)*

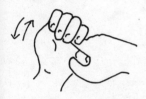

Wraps himself in his covers tight.
 (close fingers over pointer finger)
This is the way he sleeps all night.
 (rock hands back and forth)

Morning comes; he opens his eyes.
 (blink eyes)
Back with a toss, the cover flies.
 (quickly remove fingers)
Up he jumps, dresses, and is away,
 (pointer finger jumps up from palm)

Off to church on a bright Sunday.
 (make walking motion with fingers)

Night Prayer

Now I lay me down to sleep.
  (*rest cheek on palm—D.S.L. for sleep*)
Lord, hold me safely in your keep.
  (*place hands in prayer gesture*)
Your love be with me through the night,
  (*draw heart on chest—D.S.L. for heart*)
And bless me with the morning light.
  (*outstretch arms, palms up*)

God Is Love

Love, love, love, love,
The gospel in a word is love.
  (*draw heart on chest—D.S.L. for heart*)
Love your neighbor as yourself,
For God is love.
  (*sweep hands outward and
  point to self*)

Our Church

This is the roof of
the church so good.

 These are the walls
of cement and wood.

These are the windows
bright inside.

 These are the doors
that open wide.

This is the cross so
straight and tall.

Oh, what a good church building
for one and all!

(*see illustrations for actions to be followed*)

44

Peace Is the Dream

Peace is the dream; how close it seems,
When you take my hand in yours and say,
> (*clasp hands together, first right, then left
> on top; now spread hands down and out—
> D.S.L. for peace*)

"We are all people from one clay."
> (*close fingers against thumbs repeatedly—
> D.S.L. for clay*)

"We all share one earth."
> (*place the thumb and middle finger of your
> right hand on the back of the left hand near
> the wrist and rock the fingers back and
> forth—D.S.L. for earth*)

"We all share one sun."
> (*draw small circle over head—
> D.S.L. for sun*)

"May we share peace as one."
> (*repeat peace sign; then open
> arms out to others*)

Animal Adventures

Old Mr. Bullfrog

Old Mr. Bullfrog was
Sitting on a rock.
  (place fist on one knee)
Along came a little boy,
  (walk fingers along thigh)
And Mr. Bullfrog went kerplop!
  (drop fist to floor)

The Little Snail

The little snail is in no hurry.
    (*cup hand and move slowly*
    up arm to shoulder)
If he's late for school,
He doesn't worry.
    (*shake head*)
Nor have his parents ever said,
"Go to your room and make your bed."
    (*shake pointer finger*)
For he carries his bed upon his back,
He can camp anywhere with his pack.
    (*place both hands upon shoulder*)

I Caught a Fish

One, two, three, four, five,
    (*clap hands five times*)
I caught a fish alive.
    (*pretend to hold fish up*)
Six, seven, eight, nine, ten,
    (*clap five times*)
I let it go again.
    (*show empty hands*)
Why did you let it go?
Because it bit my finger so!
    (*shake hand*)
Which finger did it bite?
The little finger on the right.
    (*hold up little finger*)

My Turtle

This is my turtle.
*(place one hand over other
wiggle thumb—D.S.L. for turtle)*
He lives in a shell.
(pull thumb under hand)
He likes his home very well.
He pokes his head out when he wants to eat.
(extend thumb)
And pulls it back in when he wants to sleep.
(pull thumb under hand)

Two Blackbirds

There were two blackbirds,
Sitting on a hill.
    (*hold up both hands, thumbs
    erect and fingers bent*)
This one's named Jack.
    (*wiggle one thumb*)
This one's named Jill.
    (*wiggle other thumb*)
Fly away, Jack!
    (*hide hand behind back*)
Fly away, Jill!
    (*hide other hand behind back*)
Come back, Jack!
    (*return one hand*)
Come back, Jill!
    (*return other*)

If I Were a Horse

If I were a horse,
I'd neigh, of course.
> (*hold two fingers on either side of head
> for ears—D.S.L. for horse*)

If I were a bug,
> (*place thumb on nose with two fingers up
> as antennae—D.S.L. for insect*)

I'd curl up in a rug.
> (*hug self*)

If I were a bear,
> (*hug self and move hands down body—
> D.S.L. for bear*)

I'd comb my hair.
> (*comb hair with fingers*)

If I were a pig,
> (*puff cheeks out*)

I'd dance a jig.
> (*quickly step up and down*)

If I were a hen,
>   (*open and close index finger and*
>   *thumb in front of mouth—D.S.L. for hen*)

I'd scratch in my pen.
>   (*scratch palm with index finger of other*
>   *hand*)

If I were a lynx,
>   (*place hands at the sides of the mouth*
>   *and draw out to the sides—D.S.L. for cat*)

I'd sit like a sphinx.
>   (*hold arms out and close eyes*)

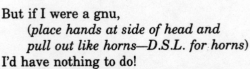

If I were a snail,
>   (*cup one hand and make it crawl*
>   *across palm of other hand*)

I'd crawl on the trail.

But if I were a gnu,
>   (*place hands at side of head and*
>   *pull out like horns—D.S.L. for horns*)

I'd have nothing to do!
>   (*shrug shoulders and raise hands*)

51

The Eensy-Weensy Spider

The eensy-weensy spider
Climbed up the waterspout.
   (*fingers climbing up—*
    try various ways)

Down came the rain
And washed the spider out.
   (*bring hands down, wiggling*
   fingers—D.S.L. for rain)

Out came the sun
And dried up all the rain.
   (*make arms arc above head*)
And the eensy-weensy spider
Climbed up the spout again.
   (*fingers climbing*)

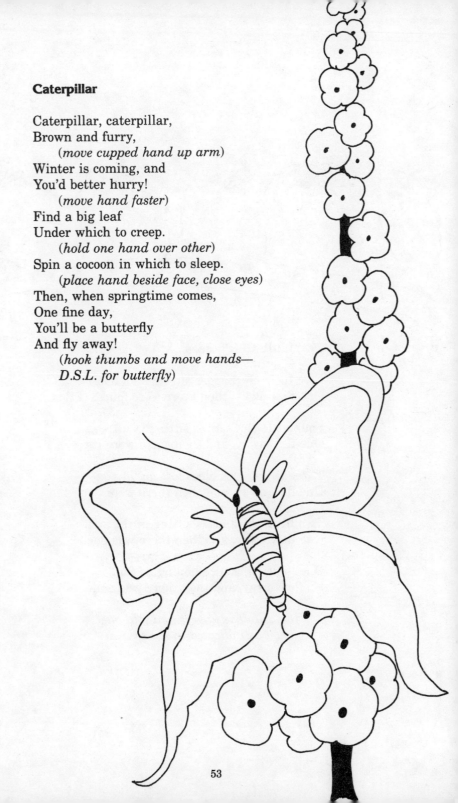

Caterpillar

Caterpillar, caterpillar,
Brown and furry,
    (move cupped hand up arm)
Winter is coming, and
You'd better hurry!
    (move hand faster)
Find a big leaf
Under which to creep.
    (hold one hand over other)
Spin a cocoon in which to sleep.
    (place hand beside face, close eyes)
Then, when springtime comes,
One fine day,
You'll be a butterfly
And fly away!
    (hook thumbs and move hands—
    D.S.L. for butterfly)

53

Five Little Chickadees

Five little chickadees sitting on a door.
One flew away; then there were four.

Four little chickadees sitting in a tree.
One flew away, and then there were three.

Three little chickadees looking at you.
One flew away, and then there were two.

Two little chickadees sitting in the sun.
One flew away, and then there was one.

One little chickadee having no fun.
He flew away, and then there was none.

*(hold up five fingers and fold one
down as indicated in the rhyme)*

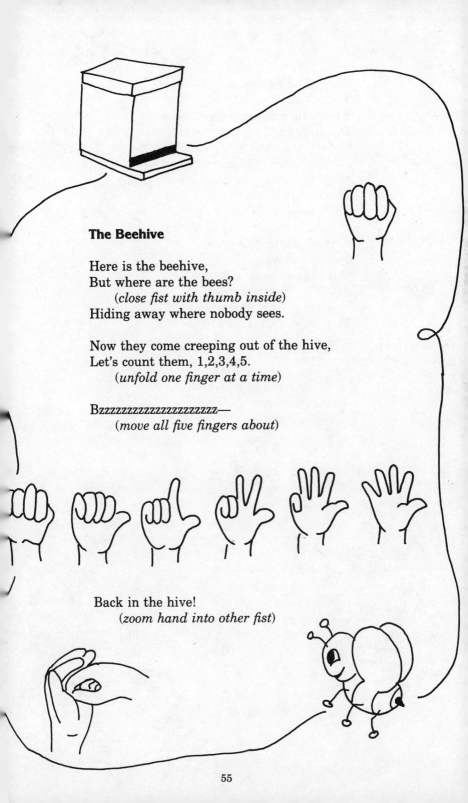

The Beehive

Here is the beehive,
But where are the bees?
   (*close fist with thumb inside*)
Hiding away where nobody sees.

Now they come creeping out of the hive,
Let's count them, 1,2,3,4,5.
   (*unfold one finger at a time*)

Bzzzzzzzzzzzzzzzzzzzzzz—
   (*move all five fingers about*)

Back in the hive!
   (*zoom hand into other fist*)

Five Little Froggies

Five little froggies sat on the shore.
One swam after a minnow.
Then there were four.
    (*move arms in swimming motion*)
Four little froggies looking out to sea.
One snapped at a fly.
Then there were three.
    (*snap hands as if to catch a fly*)
Three little froggies said,
"What will we do?"
One hopped to a toadstool,
And then there were two.
    (*hopping motion with hand*)
Two little froggies sat in the sun.
One went to sleep, and then there was one.
    (*place hand beside face; close eyes*)
One lonely froggy said, "This is no fun."
He dived into the water,
And then there was none.
    (*dive hand under arm*)

56

Bunny

Here is a bunny,
   (*make a fist*)

With ears so funny,
   (*keeping them bent, put up two fingers*)

And here is his hole in the ground.
   (*place hand on hip with arm making
   an opening*)

When a noise he hears,
He pricks up his ears!
   (*quickly extend fingers up*)

And jumps in the hole with a bound.
   (*put fist through circle made
   by hand on hip*)

Ten Little Chicks

Two little chicks looking for some more.
Along came another two, and they made four.
Four little chicks hopping over sticks.
Along came another two, and they made six.
Six little chicks perching on a gate.
Along came another two, and they made eight.
Eight little chicks ran to the pen.
Along came another two, and they made ten.
    Run to the haystack,
    Run to the pen,
    Run, little chicks,
    Back to Mother Hen.
    (hold up two fingers and add two each
    time; during the last four lines move all ten
    fingers back and forth and end by crossing
    arms and hiding hands under arms)

A Boy Went Walking

A little boy went walking
    (*walk fingers*)
One lovely summer day.
He saw a little rabbit,
    (*two fingers up*)
Who quickly hopped away.
    (*in a hopping movement
    hide hand under arm*)
He saw a shining river
Go winding in and out,
    (*made a winding
    movement with hands*)
With little fish in it,
Swimming all about.
    (*put hands together for fish and
    move back and forth*)

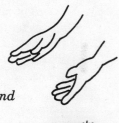

Little Grey Squirrel

The little grey squirrel searches around
    (*right hand quickly scurries about*
    looking for nuts)
To find the nuts that have fallen down.
He hunts for nuts with all his might.
Then he quickly hides them out of sight!
This is the hole where day by day,
    (*hold left hand up to make the tree,*
    making a hole with thumb and index finger)
Nut after nut he stores away.
    (*run right hand up left arm to hide*
    nuts in hole)
When winter comes, he curls up to sleep.
    (*place right hand into left*)
When he awakes, he looks for a nut to eat.
    (*scurry hand looking for nuts*)

A variation is to have nuts hidden about the room and the students search for the nuts after the fingerplay.

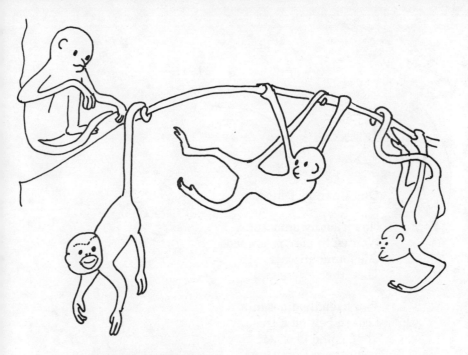

Four Little Monkeys

Two little monkeys, sitting in a tree,
Were joined by another, and that made three.
Three little monkeys in the tree did play.
They chattered and chattered in a happy way.
Three little monkeys, wishing for one more;
Another came to join them, and that made four.
Monkeys, monkeys, how many do I see?
Four little monkeys sitting in a tree.
  (*hold up appropriate number of fingers*)

Inchworm

Inchworm, inchworm moves so slow,
Up my arm you do go.
"Why do you measure me so?"
"Because so fast you do grow!"
    (*move thumb up to index
    finger; then move index
    finger out again up arm
    to the top of head*)

One Friendly Dinosaur

One friendly dinosaur
Wanted to play peek-a-boo.
She found another;
Then there were two.

Two friendly dinosaurs
Looked behind a tree.
They found another;
Then there were three.

Three friendly dinosaurs
Went to find some more.
They found another;
Then there were four.

Four friendly dinosaurs
In the water did dive.
They found another;
Then there were five.

Five friendly dinosaurs
Played in the sun.
They all ran to hide;
Now there are none.
  (*hold up appropriate number
  of fingers; then hide
  hand behind back*)

Hop like a Bunny

Hop like a bunny.
  (*hop with feet together*)
Run like a dog.
  (*walk on hands and knees*)
Walk like an elephant.
  (*hold one arm in front of face to swing
  like a trunk and sway it back and forth*)
Jump like a frog.
  (*squat down with hands on floor and
  then hop*)
Swim like a goldfish.
  (*hold palms together and move hands
  in a swimming motion*)
Fly like a bird.
  (*hold arms out and move them up and down*)
Then sit right down
And don't say a single word.
  (*sit on floor or chair*)

Five Little Bears

Five little cubby bears,
Tumbling on the ground.
    (*roll hands over*)
The first one said,
"Let's look around."
    (*hold up thumb*)
The second one said,
"See the little bunny."
    (*hold up index finger*)
The third one said,
"I smell honey."
    (*hold up middle finger
    and sniff*)
The fourth one said,
"It's over in the trees."
    (*hold up ring finger*)
The fifth one said,
"Look out! Here come the bees!"
    (*hold up little finger;
    fingers of other hand
    pretend to buzz about*)

The Bee

What do you suppose?
A bee sat on my nose!
    (*pinch nose*)
Then what do you think?
He gave me a wink.
    (*wink*)
And said, "I beg your pardon,
I thought you were the garden!"

I'm a Duck

I'm a duck—I quack, quack, quack.
   (*hook thumbs under chin,*
   circle mouth with hand, and
   open hands on each quack)
I have some feathers on my back,
   (*spread and wiggle fingers*
   at small of back, bob body
   up and down)
And when I go down to the lake,
   (*point down and make circle*
   motion with arms)
I wiggle and I waggle,
   (*raise one shoulder then other*)
And I shake, shake, shake.
   (*shake body*)
And when I go to bed at night,
   (*place head on palm*)
I always close my eyes up tight,
   (*make fists and put in front of eyes*)
And the next day when I awake,
   (*make arc over head for sun*)
I wiggle and I waggle,
And I shake, shake, shake.
   (*repeat above actions*)

May be sung to the tune:
I Like Coffee—I Like Tea.

65

Sheep So White

This is the sheep so white,
    (*make fist*)
And this is the shear so bright.
    (*hold up two fingers of*
    the other hand)
This is the way
The shepherd cut off the wool one day.
    (*run fingers over fist*)
Then he carded the wool,
Using two combs to pull and pull.
    (*run curved fingers*
    through each other)
Now the wool is spun into thread,
Dyed a bright red, and
    (*rub thumb and*
    fingers together)
Woven into cloth so fine,
And sewed for this new coat of mine.
    (*interlace fingers*)

Little Mouse

A little mouse hid in a hole.
    (*hide thumb inside fist*)
When all was quiet as quiet could be,
Out popped he!
    (*quickly bring thumb out*)
The hungry cat crept up,
To catch the mouse, you see.
    (*walk fingers of other hand down arm*)
But just as she got close,
Down went he!
    (*quickly pop thumb back into fist*)

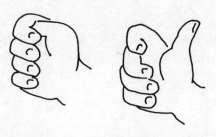

There Was a Little Turtle

There was a little turtle.
*(place one hand over the
other, wiggle thumb—D.S.L. for turtle)*

He lived in a box.
(make box with both hands)

He swam in a puddle,
*(with finger of one hand make circles
in palm of other hand)*

And he climbed on rocks.
(climb fingers over back of other hand)

He snapped at a mosquito,
(snap thumb and fingers together)

He snapped at a flea,
(repeat snap)

He snapped at a minnow,
(repeat snap)

And he snapped at me.
(point to self)

He caught the mosquito,
(clap hands)

He caught the flea,
(clap hands)

He caught the minnow,
(clap hands)

But he didn't catch me!
(point to self and shake head)

I Am an Elephant

I am an elephant so big and strong.
I swing my trunk as I walk along.
    (*swing arm in front like a
    trunk; rock back and forth*)
I can walk fast, I can walk slow,
    (*walk fast, then slowly*)
And sometimes I like to stand just so.
    (*stand on one foot and lean to side*)

Here Is the Ostrich

Here is the ostrich, straight and tall,
Nodding his head above us all.
    (*lift arm, fingers drooping,
    move hand up and down*)
But when a noise he may hear,
    (*hold hand still*)
Swish, he hides his head in fear!
    (*quickly plunge hand
    under other arm*)

The Flamingo

Be like the flamingo,
And on one leg stand.
Walk sideways like a crab,
As he scurries across the sand.
Step heavily like an elephant,
As he goes along the road.
Hop happily across the lawn,
Like the garden toad.
Now walk on tiptoe,
As slowly as cats do,
And go back to your chair,
To sit quietly like a shrew.

      (actions as indicated by rhyme)

Mr. Hushwing

Mr. Hushwing sat in a tree.
He turned his head and looked at me.
 (*circle eyes with thumbs and*
 fingers—D.S.L. for owl)
"My name is _____," I said.
 (*point to self and say name*)
He winked an eye, and away he flew,
 (*wink eye and close one*
 hand around eye)
Asking as he went, "Who, who, who?"
 (*move arms up and down*)

(*I use this rhyme during storytime.*
My puppet, Mr. Hushwing, helps
introduce me and the stories.)

70

Baby Kangaroo

Jump, jump, jump,
Goes the big kangaroo.
> (*hold index finger
> up; hide thumb
> under other fingers;
> move hand up
> and down*)

I thought there was one,
But I see there are two!
> (*bring thumb out*)

The mother takes her young one
Along in a pouch
> (*return thumb under fingers*)

Where he can nap like a child
On a couch.
> (*again move hand up and down*)

71

Friends and Family

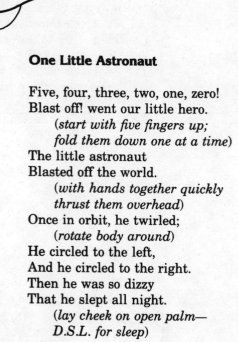

One Little Astronaut

Five, four, three, two, one, zero!
Blast off! went our little hero.
    (*start with five fingers up;*
    fold them down one at a time)
The little astronaut
Blasted off the world.
    (*with hands together quickly*
    thrust them overhead)
Once in orbit, he twirled;
    (*rotate body around*)
He circled to the left,
And he circled to the right.
Then he was so dizzy
That he slept all night.
    (*lay cheek on open palm—*
    D.S.L. for sleep)

The Fine Family

This is the family in my household.
    (*hold up all five fingers*)
Some are young,
    (*move thumb*)
Some are old,
    (*move index finger*)
Some are tall,
    (*move middle finger*)
Some are small, and
    (*move ring finger*)
Some are growing, like me.
    (*move little finger*)
We all live together as a family.
    (*move all fingers*)

Houses

Here is the nest for robin.
(cup hands together)

Here is a hive for the bee.
(fists together)

Here is a hole for the bunny.
(finger and thumb make a circle)

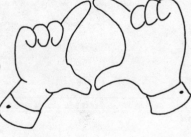

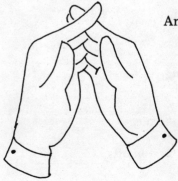

And here is a house for me!
(fingertips together)

Grandma's Glasses

Here are grandma's glasses.
    (*fingers around eyes*)

Here is grandma's hat.
    (*hands on head*)

And this is the way she
Folds her hands,
And lays them in her lap.
    (*fold hands and place in lap*)

Here are grandpa's glasses.
    (*repeat above action*)

Here is grandpa's hat.
    (*repeat above action*)

And this is the way he folds his arms,
Just like that!
    (*cross arms in front of chest*)

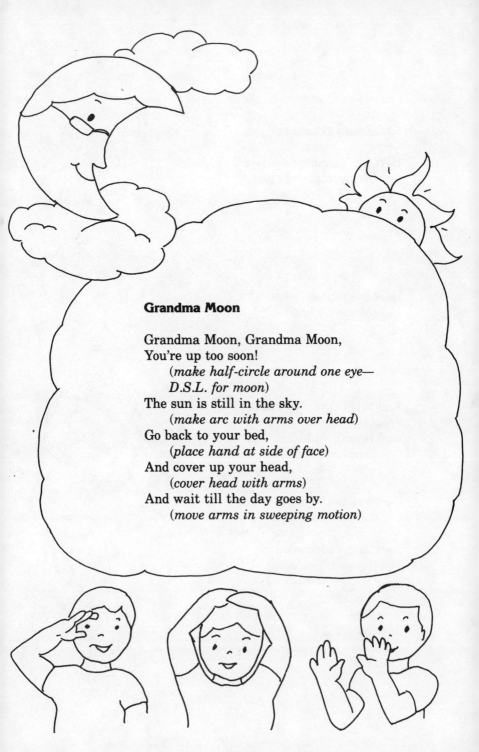

Grandma Moon

Grandma Moon, Grandma Moon,
You're up too soon!
    (*make half-circle around one eye—*
    D.S.L. for moon)
The sun is still in the sky.
    (*make arc with arms over head*)
Go back to your bed,
    (*place hand at side of face*)
And cover up your head,
    (*cover head with arms*)
And wait till the day goes by.
    (*move arms in sweeping motion*)

Five at the Table

Five at the table, sitting by the door.
One goes to work;
Then there are four.

Four at the table, happy as can be.
One goes to plant a garden;
Then there are three.

Three at the table; what can we do?
One goes shopping;
Then there are two.

Two at the table, sitting in the sun.
One goes to school;
Then there is one.

One at the table, a tired little hero.
He goes to take a nap;
Then there is zero.
> (*hold up five fingers and then
> fold them down one at a time*)

Dentist

If I were a dentist,
    (*point to self*)
I know what I would do.
    (*nod head*)
I'd tell all the children,
"Brush your teeth,
    (*pretend to brush*)
To keep your smile like new."
    (*smile*)
And if a tiny hole should show,
    (*make circle with fingers*)
I'd say, "Climb in my chair."
I'd make my little drill go
Buzzzzzzzzz.
I'd put a filling there.
    (*point to teeth*)

Barber

I hop into the barber's chair
    (*sit on chair*)
And let the barber cut my hair.
    (*point to hair*)
"Zzzzzzzz," the barber's clippers go,
    (*pretend to cut hair*)
Sometimes fast and sometimes slow.
    (*move hand fast, then slowly*)
I like it at our barber shop
Because I get a lollipop!
    (*pretend to lick lollipop*)

Fire Fighter

Ten little fire fighters,
Sleeping in a row.
  (*hold up ten fingers*)
Ding! goes the bell,
  (*pretend to pull bell*)
And down the pole they go.
  (*cross arms, bend knees*)
Off on the engine, oh, oh, oh,
  (*pretend to steer*)
Using the big hose, so, so, so.
  (*pretend to hold hose*)
When all the fire is out, home they go.
  (*pretend to steer engine*)
Back to bed, all in a row.
  (*hold up ten fingers*)

Police Officer

Police officers are helpers,
Wherever they may stand,
They tell us when to stop and go,
By holding up their hands.
  (*one child may give stop-and-
  go signals for the others*)

Traffic Light

Red on top,
>   (*index finger strokes lips—
>   D.S.L. for red*)

Green below,
>   (*point index finger and move hand
>   to the right with a shaking motion—
>   D.S.L. for green*)

Yellow in the middle,
>   (*put little finger and thumb up and
>   move hand to the right with a
>   shaking motion—D.S.L. for yellow*)

But no riddle!
>   (*shake head no*)

Red means stop.
>   (*hold hand up palm out*)

Green means go.
>   (*roll index fingers
>   around each other—
>   D.S.L. for go*)

Yellow means wait,
Even if you're late!
>   (*shake index finger
>   as if scolding*)

Mother's Knives and Forks

Here are mother's knives and forks.
   (*interlock fingers, palms up*)
This is father's table.
   (*interlock fingers, palms down*)
This is sister's looking-glass.
   (*make circle with index fingers and thumbs*)
And this is baby's cradle.
   (*rock hands back and forth*)

Birthday Parade

A birthday parade! Oh, what fun!
A birthday parade; everyone come!
Make some music anyway you can.
Come join us in our birthday band.
Clap your hands or beat a drum.
Come join us in our birthday fun.
March, march, march! As we march,
   make a ring
Around the birthday child; so we can sing—
   (*sing happy-birthday-to-you song and use
   rhythm instruments as you march around
   the birthday child*)

Toys and Tools

The Kite

Blow, little wind, on my kite.
    (*blow through hands*)
Carry it high out of sight.
    (*hand over eyes*)
Now blow, little wind, on that tree
    (*blow through hands*)
And shake my kite down to me!
    (*shake hands back and forth*)

Johnny's Hammers

(Johnny)* works with one hammer,
One hammer, one hammer.
(Johnny) works with one hammer,
All morning long.
   (*pound right hand on knee*)

(Johnny) works with two hammers,
Two hammers, two hammers.
(Johnny) works with two hammers,
All afternoon long.
   (*pound both fists on knees*)

(Johnny) works with three hammers,
Three hammers, three hammers,
(Johnny) works with three hammers,
All evening long.
   (*tap right foot along with fists*)

(Johnny) works with four hammers,
Four hammers, four hammers.
(Johnny) works with four hammers,
All night long.
   (*tap both feet along with fists*)

(Johnny) works with five hammers,
Five hammers, five hammers.
(Johnny) works with five hammers;
Then he goes to sleep.
   (*move head back and forth
   along with other action;
   then put cheek on palm*)

*Change Johnny to girl's name every other time.

Jack-in-the-Box

Jack-in-the-box all closed up tight.
Not any air, not any light.
　　(squat down as small as possible)
My, but it's dark down here in a heap.
Let's open the lid, and up we leap!
　　(jump up to a standing position)

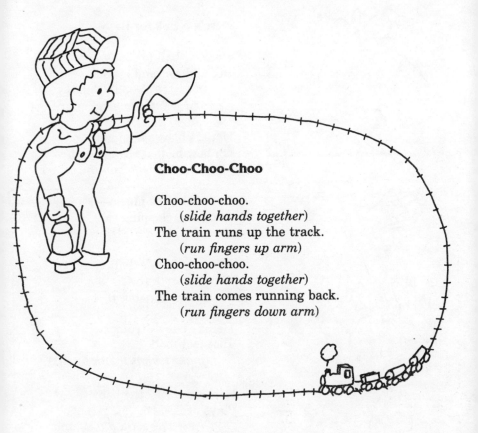

Choo-Choo-Choo

Choo-choo-choo.
  (*slide hands together*)
The train runs up the track.
  (*run fingers up arm*)
Choo-choo-choo.
  (*slide hands together*)
The train comes running back.
  (*run fingers down arm*)

Robot, Robot

Robot, robot, do as I command!
Robot, robot, lift your right hand.
Robot, robot, touch your nose.
Robot, robot, wiggle your toes.
Robot, robot, turn slowly around.
Robot, robot, touch the ground.
Robot, robot, is quiet as can be.
Robot, robot, needs a new battery.
  (*follow actions as rhyme indicates*)

*A variation is to play the
game like "Simon Says."*

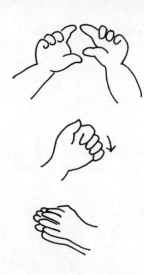

Here's a Ball for Baby

Here's a ball for baby,
Big and soft and round!
    (*make circle with thumbs
    and pointer fingers*)

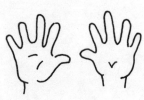

Here is baby's hammer,
Oh how he [she] can pound!
    (*pound one fist on the other*)

Here is baby's music—
Clapping, clapping so!
    (*clap hands*)

Here are baby's dollies,
Standing in a row.
    (*ten fingers open*)

Here is baby's trumpet,
Toot-toot-toot!
    (*make trumpet with hands*)

Here's the way the baby
Plays peek-a-boo.
    (*cover face with hands and
    peek out between fingers*)

Here's a big umbrella
To keep the baby dry.
    (*make umbrella with hand*)

Here's the way the baby
Goes a-lulla-bye.
    (*make rocking motion with hands*)

The Box

Here is a box.
    (*make a fist*)
Put on a lid.
    (*place other hand on top*)
Can you guess what is hid?
    (*peek under hand*)
Why, it's a _____without
Any doubt!
    (*add any word desired*)
Open the box and let it out!
    (*remove lid and make sound
    appropriate for object*)

Counting Balls

Here's a ball,
    (*put thumb and index finger together
    to make a circle*)

And here's a ball,
    (*put both hands together*)

And here's a great big ball I see.
    (*make circle with arms*)

Shall we count them?
Are you ready?
One, two, three.
    (*remake each ball as counting*)

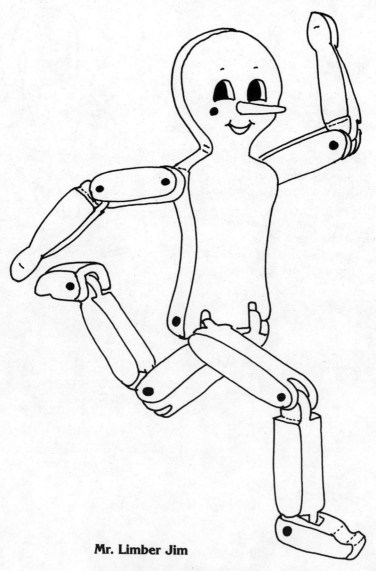

Mr. Limber Jim

Oh, the Limber Jim is a jolly, jolly man.
He jumps and jumps as fast as he can.
    (*jump up and down*)
His arms fly out, and his legs do too.
    (*raise arms and one leg*)
Mr. Limber Jim, how do you do?
    (*bow to person next to you*)

In the Garden

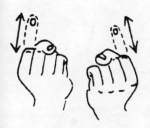

Popcorn

Popcorn, popping, pop, pop, pop!
> (*with palms toward you and fingers bent,*
> *pop up index fingers alternately*
> *—D.S.L. for popcorn*)

Look out! It's pushing over the top.
> (*lift arms overhead and then put them down*)

How can a kernel so hard and small
> (*close hands into fists*)

Explode into a tiny snowball?
> (*open fists quickly*)

Sleeping Flowers

Let's play we are little flowers,
Sleeping in a row.
 (*close eyes and drop head to hands*)
Now we'll raise our head,
Stretch our arms,
And nod in the breeze just so.
 (*motion as indicated in rhyme*)

The Flower

Here's a green leaf,
 (*show one hand*)

And here's a green leaf.
 (*show other hand*)

That, you see, makes two.

Here is a bud
 (*cup hands together*)

That makes a flower.
Watch it bloom for you!
 (*gradually open hands*)

Two Little Apples

Way up high in the apple tree,
  (*hold both arms up*)

Two little apples smiled at me.
  (*point to self*)

So I shook that tree
As hard as I could.
  (*shake hands back and forth*)

Down came the apples!
  (*hands flutter downward*)

Ummmmm, were they good!
  (*rub tummy*)

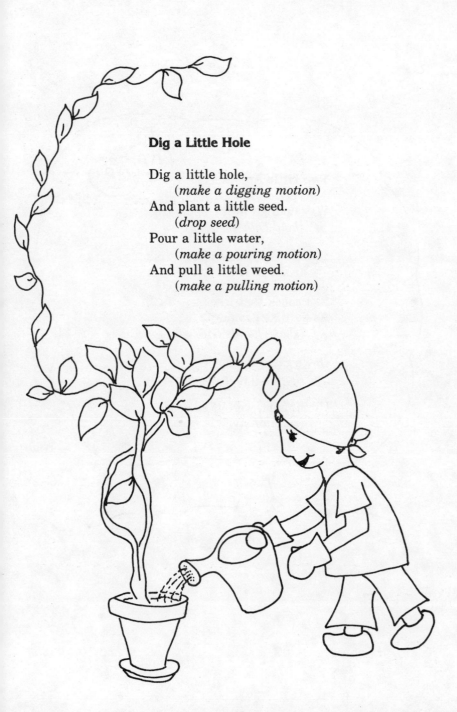

Dig a Little Hole

Dig a little hole,
   (*make a digging motion*)
And plant a little seed.
   (*drop seed*)
Pour a little water,
   (*make a pouring motion*)
And pull a little weed.
   (*make a pulling motion*)

Little Seeds

I put some little flower seeds
    (hold cupped hand up)
Down in the warm, soft ground.
    (stoop down, pretend to plant seed)
I sprinkled them with water
From a sprinkling can I found.
    (pretend to water the area)
The big, round sun shone brightly.
    (make an arc with hands and arms)
We had some soft rain showers.
    (flutter fingers downward)
The little seeds began to grow.
Soon I had lovely flowers.
    *(stoop down and slowly
    stand, opening arms)*

Hurrah for Holidays

Five Little Jack-o'-Lanterns

Five little jack-o'-lanterns sitting on a gate.
First one said, "Oh my, it's getting late."
Second one said, "There are witches in the air."
Third one said, "Oh, we don't care."
Fourth one said, "Let's run and run and run."
Fifth one said, "It's Halloween fun."
    (*hold fingers up and move one at a time*)
Wooooooooooooooooo went the wind,
And out went the light!
    (*clap hands*)
Five little jack-o'-lanterns rolled out of sight.
    (*hide hands behind back*)

Halloween Witches

One little, two little, three little witches
  (*hold up hand, move fingers at count*)
Fly over haystacks, fly over ditches,
  (*fly hand in an up-and-down motion*)
Slide down moonbeams without any hitches.
  (*glide hand downward*)
Heigh-ho, Halloween's here!

May be sung to the tune: "One Little Indian."

Don't Let the Goblins Get You!

The witches are riding tonight!
  (*pretend to hold brooms and circle about
  room; may repeat three times*)
The old black cat is looking for a fight!
  (*walk on tiptoe; hold hands like claws*)
The bats are flying all over the sky.
  (*cross hands at wrists with thumbs held in
  palms; flap like wings—D.S.L. for bat*)
Don't let the goblins get you.
Oh my, oh me, oh my!
  (*point at each other*)

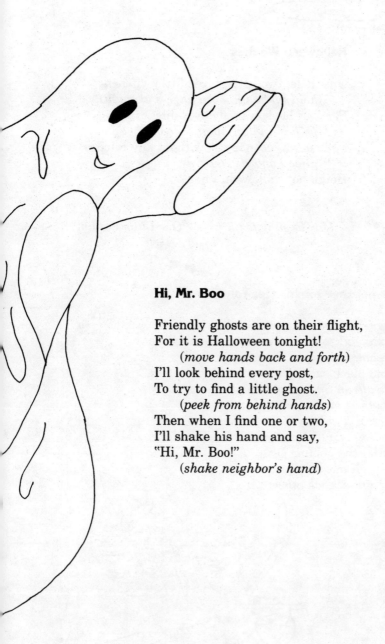

Hi, Mr. Boo

Friendly ghosts are on their flight,
For it is Halloween tonight!
   (*move hands back and forth*)
I'll look behind every post,
To try to find a little ghost.
   (*peek from behind hands*)
Then when I find one or two,
I'll shake his hand and say,
"Hi, Mr. Boo!"
   (*shake neighbor's hand*)

If I Were a Witch

If I were a witch,
  (*hold bent fingers
  near face*)
I'd ride on a broom,
  (*pretend to hold broom*)
And scatter the ghosts
With a zoom, zoom, zoom!
  (*quickly sweep hands
  back and forth*)

Scary Eyes

I'm a scary ghost.
See my big and scary eyes?
  (*circle eyes with thumbs
  and index fingers*)
Look out now for a big surprise.
BOO!
  (*quickly remove hands*)

Jack-o'-Lantern

Sometimes big and sometimes small,
But always round and yellow.
> (*make a large and then a small circle
> with arms and fingers*)

When children fix my famous grin,
> (*show teeth*)

Then I'm a scary fellow!
> (*make a scary face*)

Thanksgiving Turkey

The little (girl/boy) went to look
> (*hold hand above eyes*)

To find a turkey for the cook.
The turkey spread his wings out wide
> (*move arms as if wings*)

And flew into a tree to hide.
> (*place hands over face*)

"Gobble, gobble, gobble," said he.
"They won't make a Thanksgiving
feast of me!"
> (*point to self and shake head*)

98

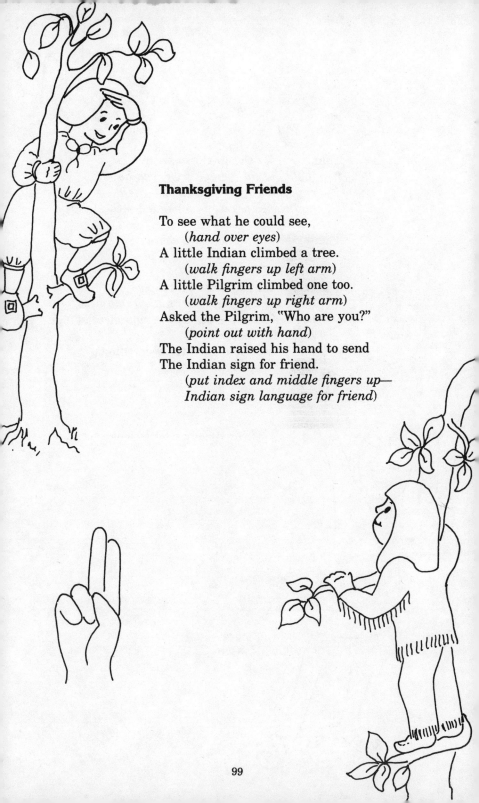

Thanksgiving Friends

To see what he could see,
  (*hand over eyes*)
A little Indian climbed a tree.
  (*walk fingers up left arm*)
A little Pilgrim climbed one too.
  (*walk fingers up right arm*)
Asked the Pilgrim, "Who are you?"
  (*point out with hand*)
The Indian raised his hand to send
The Indian sign for friend.
  (*put index and middle fingers up—
  Indian sign language for friend*)

Thank You

Thank you for the world so sweet;
   (hold out three fingers on each hand;
   right hand circles around the left
   and comes to rest on top of left—(D.S.L. for
   world)
Thank you for the food we eat;
   (hand goes to mouth as if placing food in
   mouth—D.S.L. for food)
Thank you for the birds that sing;
   (hold right index finger and thumb in
   front of mouth; close as the movement of a
   beak—D.S.L. for bird)
      Thank you, God, for everything.
         (open arms wide)

Birthday

(Name of child) had a birthday.
(Name) had a cake.
    (*make circle with arms*)
(Name's) mother made it.
    (*make a stirring motion*)
(Name) watched it bake.

Frosting on the top,
    (*hold right hand out*)
Frosting in between.
    (*hold left hand under right hand*)
Oh, it was the nicest cake
That you have ever seen.

(Name) had some candles.
Count them now with me—
1,2,3,4,5. Who can tell me
How many years (name) has been alive?
    (or)
1,2,3,4. That's all, no more.

Chimney

Here is the chimney.
    (*clench hand*)
Here is the top.
    (*put other hand on top*)
Open the lid,
    (*remove top hand*)
And out Santa will pop!
    (*pop up thumb*)

Five Little Bells

Five little bells hanging in a row,
    (*hold up five fingers*)
First one said, "Ring me slow."
    (*move thumb slowly*)
Second one said, "Ring me fast!"
    (*move index finger quickly*)
Third one said, "Ring me last."
    (*move middle finger*)
Fourth one said, "I'm like a chime."
    (*move ring finger*)
Fifth one said, "Ring us all at Christmastime."
    (*wiggle all five fingers*)

Christmastime

Ring, ring, ring the bells,
    (move hand as if ringing bell—
    D.S.L. for bell)
Ring them loud and clear.
To tell the children everywhere
That Christmastime is here.
    (with palms out make arc from left
    to right—D.S.L. for Christmas)

May sing to the tune:
Row, Row, Row Your Boat.

Santa Claus

Down the chimney dear Santa crept
  *(hold left arm up and creep fingers
  of right hand down it)*
Into the room while the children all slept.
  *(close eyes and put one hand on
  palm of other hand)*
He saw their stockings hung in a row,
  (place hand over eyes as if searching)
And he packed gifts into each toe.
  (make motions as if filling stockings)
Although he counted them, one, two, three,
  (bring three fingers out one at a time)
The baby's stocking he could not see.
"Ho, ho!" said Santa, "That won't do."
  (hold tummy and laugh)
So he popped her present right into her shoe.
  *(cup left hand and put right hand
  into it—D.S.L. for shoe)*

Little Christmas Tree

I'm a little Christmas tree.
    (*hold hands outstretched*)
I'm standing by the door.
    (*stand up very straight*)
And I'm so full of presents,
I can't hold any more.
    (*shake head*)
I'm just a little Christmas tree.
    (*stretch hands out*)
Up here there is a star.
    (*put hands over head*)
I have many good gifts, too,
Like the wise men from afar.
    (*hold hand above eyes as if looking*)

Birthday Star

Twinkle, twinkle,
Birthday star,
Atop our Christmas tree.
    (*slide index fingers up past
    each other—D.S.L. for star*)

Twinkle, twinkle,
Jesus' star,
Shining with love for me.
    (*draw heart on chest—
    D.S.L. for heart*)

Five Little Valentines

Five little valentines all in place,
And each one has a different face.
This one is lacy.
This one is frilly.
This one is funny.
This one is silly.
But some are special too.
    (*hold up five fingers*
    and move one at a time)
This one says, "I love you."
    (*point to child*)

Fourth of July

United States has a birthday.
Each Fourth of July it comes.
    (*hold up four fingers*)
I love to see the parade
    (*hold hand above eyes*)
And listen for the drums.
    (*pretend to beat drum—*
    D.S.L. for drum)

Bunny, Hippity-Hoppity-Hip

Here comes a bunny, hippity-hoppity-hip.
    (place hands on hips; hop three times)
His long ears flip, flop, flip.
    (put index and middle fingers up at side
    of head, palms back—D.S.L. for rabbit)
His nose goes twink, twink, twink.
    (twitch nose three times)
His eyes go wink, wink, wink.
    (point to eye and wink three times)
Stroke his coat so soft and furry.
    (stroke arm)
Hippity-hoppity-hip, off he goes in a hurry!
    (hop three times)

Easter Eggs

Easter eggs here,
Easter eggs there,
Easter eggs everywhere!
    (point to various areas)
I look under.
    (look under hand)
I look behind.
    (look behind an object)
So many eggs I find.
    (hold up cupped hands)

The Spell of Seasons

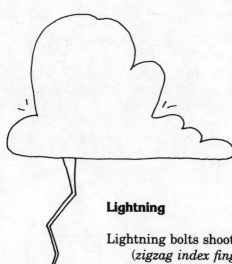

Lightning

Lightning bolts shoot from the cloud.
   (*zigzag index finger down—*
   D.S.L. for lightning)
Cover your ears; the thunder is loud!
   (*hold hands over ears*)
Hail and rain will soon be here.
   (*bring hands down, wiggling fingers—*
   D.S.L. for rain)
Our dog hides under the bed in fear.
   (*cover head with arms*)

The Old Scarecrow

The old scarecrow is such a funny man.
He flops in the wind as hard as he can.
He flops to the left, and he flops to the right.
He flops back and forth with all his might.
His arms swing out; his legs swing too.
He nods his head in a "How-do-you-do?"
While the flock of hungry crows,
Eat the corn and enjoy the shows!
　　(*actions as indicated by rhyme*)

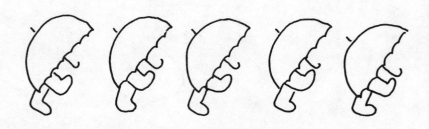

Umbrella Parade

Drip, drop, drip,
*(fluttering fingers
bring hands down—
D.S.L. for rain)*
Spring rain has come no doubt.

Drip, drop, drip,
(repeat above action)
Making puddles all about.
(draw circle in air)

Drip, drop, drip,
(repeat first action)
I know why puddles are made.
(shake head yes)

Drip, drop, drip,
(repeat first action)
For an umbrella parade.
*(hold pointer finger up and
place other hand over it)*

Rainbow

Purple, blue, green, yellow,
Orange, and red,
  (*hold one finger up at a time or
  use the D.S.L. for each color*)
Six colors in a bow overhead.
  (*make an arc with arms*)
Sunshine peeking through the rain
In the sky,
  (*peek through fingers*)
Make the rainbow I see up so high.
  (*point upward*)

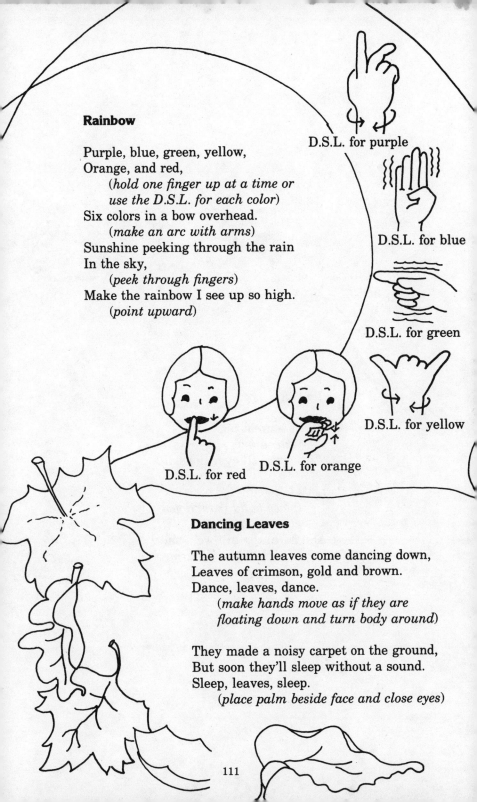

D.S.L. for purple

D.S.L. for blue

D.S.L. for green

D.S.L. for yellow

D.S.L. for red

D.S.L. for orange

Dancing Leaves

The autumn leaves come dancing down,
Leaves of crimson, gold and brown.
Dance, leaves, dance.
  (*make hands move as if they are
  floating down and turn body around*)

They made a noisy carpet on the ground,
But soon they'll sleep without a sound.
Sleep, leaves, sleep.
  (*place palm beside face and close eyes*)

Big Hill

Here's a great big hill,
(*extend arm sideways*)
With snow all over the side.

Let's take our sleds,
(*place hand palm down
on shoulder*)
And down the hill we'll slide!
(*slide hand down arm*)

Snowman

I built a snowman, fat and round.
    (*place one fist on the other*)
Then the sunlight came beaming down.
    (*place arms over head in an arc*)
The sunlight shown brightly on the snow.
Now where did my snowman go?
    (*put palms up in questioning manner*)

Old Jack Frost

Old Jack Frost came last night.
(hug self and shiver)
He's looking for my ears to bite,
(pinch ears)
And he wants to bite my toes.
(touch toes)
Oh no! Look out! He wants my nose!
(quickly cover nose)

Snowflakes

Snowflakes whirling all around,
(hands flutter down as person turns around)
Until they cover all the ground.
(children sink slowly to the floor)
But when the sun comes out to play,
(make an arc with arms)
Then the snowflakes melt away.
(lie flat on floor and pretend to melt)

Winter Fun

It bites your toes
    (touch toes)
And nips your nose,
    (pinch nose)
Watch out your ears don't freeze!
    (cover ears with hands)
It makes you shiver; it makes you quiver,
    (hold self and shake)
And sometimes makes you sneeze.
    (pretend to sneeze)
It makes you hurry,
It makes you scurry,
And makes you want to run.
But we remember most
    (move hands quickly back and forth)
How we like to skate and coast
    (slide hand down arm)
And think that winter's fun!
    (shake head yes)

Mitten Weather

Thumb in the thumb place,
Fingers all together.
This is the rhyme we say,
In mitten weather.
    (hold fingers together
    and thumb apart)
Fingers in the wide part,
Thumb stands all alone.
Mittens keep fingers warm,
When the cold winds moan.
    (blow through hands
    make "Ooooo" sound)

Index

Subject Index